This book belongs to:

....

For Eunice, who loves dogs!
With love and thanks G.S.

To perfect pets everywhere,
with love C.J.

HODDER CHILDREN'S BOOKS
First published in Great Britain in 2013 by Hodder and Stoughton
This edition first published in 2014

Text copyright © Gillian Shields, 2013
Illustrations copyright © Cally Johnson-Isaacs, 2013

A CIP catalogue record for this book is available from the British Library.

ISBN: 978 1 44494 711 3

1 3 5 7 9 10 8 6 4 2

Printed and bound in China

MIX
Paper from
responsible sources
FSC® C104740
FSC
www.fsc.org

Hodder Children's Books
An imprint of Hachette Children's Group
Part of Hodder and Stoughton
Carmelite House, 50 Victoria Embankment,
London, EC4Y 0DZ

An Hachette UK Company
www.hachette.co.uk

www.hachettechildrens.co.uk

THAT DOG!

Gillian Shields and Cally Johnson-Isaacs

Hodder
Children's
Books

The mean miserable Jones family never took any notice
of their dog, even though he was just bursting to be loved.

'That dog is so lazy,' said Mr Jones.

But he never took that dog for a walk.

'That dog is so smelly,' said Mrs Jones. But she never gave that dog a bath.

'That dog is so boring,' said Jo and Josephine Jones. But they never played with that dog. All they ever did was quarrel and fight, quarrel and fight.

And so **that dog** was sad, sad, sad. He lay on the ground and howled as though the end of the world had come.

Then he stopped. There was no point in crying, oh no.
That dog jumped up.

'I'll show them,' he thought. 'I'll make them take notice!'
That made him feel better, oh yes it did.

So one night, when Mr Jones and Mrs Jones
and Jo and Josephine Jones were all asleep,
that dog packed his bag, put on his best scarf
and crept out of the house. Creep, creep, creep.

And he ran away.

He ran away over here.

He ran away
over there.

After a while, he felt hungry.
But there was no one to feed him,
not even mean moody Mr Jones.

That dog got hungrier
and hungrier. 'I'll have to get
a job,' he said.
So he did.

That dog worked hard. Oh, he worked so hard, oh yes! He washed up a **million** plates in a restaurant.

He drove a taxi here and there,

there and here.

He mucked
out the stables.

Muck, muck, muck.

He picked up litter in the park.
Little by little, people began to notice him...

Pick, pick, pick.

That dog was always the first one to help old ladies across the road. He liked helping people.

So he learned to be a
fire fighter and a nurse...

...and a helicopter rescue pilot,

and a car mechanic,

and a farmer,

That dog never gave up! He even went to the library and read every single book, until he knew **everything.** EVEN...

...how to make new friends.

When the Jones family finally noticed **that dog** on TV they grumbled, 'That's our dog!'

But **that dog** didn't need the mean miserable Jones family anymore, oh no.

Because at the end of a hard day's work, he knew just

where to find the people that loved him the most.
Because that dog...

THAT DOG – was
AMAZING!

Fabulous books from this talented team:

978 1 444 90403 1

Gillian Shields and Cally Johnson-Isaacs

THAT DOG!

He's no ordinary dog!

978 1 444 90401 7

Gillian Shields and Cally Johnson-Isaacs

Elephantantrum

Mind your manners - elephant style!